espresso
education

Phonics

Bad Luck, Sal!

Diane Marwood

D0235125

First published in 2011 by
Franklin Watts
338 Euston Road
London NW1 3BH

Franklin Watts Australia
Level 17/207 Kent Street
Sydney NSW 2000

Text and illustration © Franklin Watts 2011

The Espresso characters are originated and
designed by Claire Underwood and Pesky Ltd.

The Espresso characters are the property of
Espresso Education Ltd.

All rights reserved.

A CIP catalogue record for this book is
available from the British Library.

ISBN: 978 1 4451 0423 2 (hbk)
ISBN: 978 1 4451 0436 2 (pbk)

Illustrations by Artful Doodlers Ltd.
Art Director: Jonathan Hair
Series Editor: Jackie Hamley
Series Designer: Matthew Lilly

Printed in China

Franklin Watts is a division of
Hachette Children's Books,
an Hachette UK company.

www.hachette.co.uk

Level 1 50 words
Concentrating on CVC words plus and, the, to

Level 2 70 words
Concentrating on double letter sounds and new letter
sounds (ck, ff, ll, ss, j, v, w, x, y, z, zz) plus no, go, I

Level 3 100 words
Concentrating on new graphemes (qu, ch, sh, th, ng,
ai, ee, igh, oa, oo, ar, or, ur, ow, oi, ear, air, ure, er)
plus he, she, we, me, be, was, my, you, they, her, all

Level 4 150 words
Concentrating on adjacent consonants (CVCC/CCVC
words) plus said, so, have, like, some, come, were, there,
little, one, do, when, out, what

Sal had a go.

Sal got a doll.

Can Sal pick the doll up?

No! The doll
fell back.

7

Sal had a go.
Sal got a big bug.
Can Sal pick the
bug up?

No! The bug
fell back.

Kim had a go.

Kim got the doll
and the big bug.

bell

lick

doll

fell

tell

suck

tick

pick

wick

roll

tuck

luck

well

Answers

dolls-doll, sticks-stick, slick-lick, wick
tell-bell-fell-well, luck-suck-tuck

Espresso Connections

This book may be used in conjunction with the Literacy area on Espresso to secure children's phonics learning. Here are some suggestions.

Word Machine
Encourage children to play the Word Machine Level 1. Demonstrate how the machine works, and then move on to the activities.

Ask children to find the correct first letter.
Then ask children to find the correct last letter.
Then ask children to find the correct middle letter.

Check that children are able to hear the difference between the letter sounds as different words come up.

Praise plausible attempts, such as substituting the letter "k" for "c" when attempting to find the hard c sound.

Finally, ask children to find all the letters of the word.

Spot the Word
Choose a book from the Big Book selection, for example **"Places we like to visit"** to play Spot the Word.

Give children pieces of paper with the high frequency words **and** or **the** or **to** or **I**. (The class could be split, with groups of children looking for different words.)

Ask children to note down on the paper each time they have seen or heard the word they are looking for.

At the end of the book, children should count up how many times their target word has been used.

Go back through the book together and see whether they got it right.

Praise plausible attempts, for example "they" for "the" and take the opportunity to point out why these words are different.

You could replicate the activity with this phonics story.